Days

WRITTEN BY
Patricia MacLachlan

ILLUSTRATED BY
Micha Archer

Where I was born, there was a sky
so big, there was no end of it.
The summer mornings were cool,
and the sun rose orange.

Where I was born, the earth smelled of cattle and bluegrass and hyssop.

When I lay down in the fields next to my farm,
I could smell Mama's wild roses that grew
next to the hollyhocks.

There were small towns with names we loved—
Sunrise, Rattlesnake, Chugwater, and Spotted Horse.

There were filling stations where
Papa put gas
into his old gray car,

and we got drinks
out of cold-water lift-top tanks.

There were prairie birds—
grouse,
scissortails,
magpies,
and dippers
in the rushing streams
where the prairie
met the mountains.

There were farm horses to ride—
Lyddie
and Blue
and Joe—
who we galloped on dirt roads
and across fields
and over fences.
Who pulled the plows
and wagons.

We rode the filled wagon
to the tall granary
by the railroad,
buried in grain
that sneaked into our pockets and
the cuffs of our jeans.

There were farm dogs
who slept on the wooden porches when they weren't working—

Duke and Skippy
and three-legged May,
who kept up with them.

And worker dogs herded the cattle and sheep—
    nipping,
        barking,
            circling
to keep the herds safe from coyotes
and wolves.

Bucky and Prince
were brave dogs
who ate well
and slept well
and loved their work.

In the heat of summer
we swam in the farm pond,
floating,
spitting streams
of water
high into the blue sky.

Sometimes we drove to town
to buy the cloth Mama wanted,
the tools for Papa,
and pencils
and penny mints for us.

There were cowboys in town—
some of them were poets—
who said,
"Hello, little lady," to Mama.

They had dogs, too,
who sat patiently in the beds
of their trucks
outside diners
where the cowboys ate and drank.

When we drove home
we saw prairie dogs
sitting by their holes—
watching us
before they plunged
          down
     under the earth again.

And when the day was over,
and it was dusk,
we played kick the can—
hidden behind sheds and bushes,
laughing,
shrieking,

rushing out
to kick the can
in the middle of the dirt road,
Half frightened
when the darkness came.

We never stopped until
mothers and fathers,
aunts and uncles,
or grandparents
came out of their houses to
bring us in for bed . . .

where we read under quilts of
stars,
pinwheels,
squares,
with our flashlights. . . .

Until we fell asleep. And the summer moon rose yellow.

For my family—past and present.—P. M.

Dedicated to my sister.—M. A.

MARGARET K. McELDERRY BOOKS
An Imprint of Simon & Schuster Children's Publishing Division
1230 Avenue of the Americas, New York, New York 10020
Text copyright © 2020 by Patricia MacLachlan
Illustrations copyright © 2020 by Micha Archer
MARGARET K. McELDERRY BOOKS is a trademark of Simon & Schuster, Inc.
For information about special discounts for bulk purchases, please contact Simon &
Schuster Special Sales at 1-866-506-1949 or business@simonandschuster.com.
The Simon & Schuster Speakers Bureau can bring authors to your live event. For more
information or to book an event, contact the Simon & Schuster Speakers Bureau at
1-866-248-3049 or visit our website at www.simonspeakers.com.
Book design by Debra Sfetsios-Conover
The text for this book was set in Celestia Antiqua std.
The collage illustrations were done with a combination of acrylics, inks, and textured
papers that Micha creates with origami and tissue papers and homemade stamps.
Manufactured in China
0320 SCP
First Edition
10 9 8 7 6 5 4 3 2 1
Library of Congress Cataloging-in-Publication Data
Names: MacLachlan, Patricia, author. | Archer, Micha, illustrator.
Title: Prairie days / Patricia MacLachlan ; illustrated by Micha Archer.
Description: First edition. | New York : Margaret K. McElderry Books, [2020] |
Summary: Describes summer days growing up on the prairie.
Identifiers: LCCN 2018052580 | ISBN 9781442441910 (hardcover) |
ISBN 9781442441927 (eBook)
Subjects: | CYAC: Prairies—Fiction.
Classification: LCC PZ7.M2225 Pr 2020 | DDC [E]—dc23
LC record available at https://lccn.loc.gov/2018052580